Hunnypot

A Party for

Winnie-the-Pooh

From the Stories by A.A. Milne

With new and adapted illustrations
in the style of E.H. Shepard

METHUEN

One day, when the sun had come back over the Forest, and all the streams of the Forest were tinkling happily to find themselves their own pretty shape again, the little pools lay dreaming of the life they had seen and the big things they had done. In the warmth and quiet of the Forest, wood-pigeons were complaining gently to themselves in their lazy comfortable way that it was the other fellow's fault, but it didn't matter very much. On such a day as this Christopher Robin whistled in a special way he had, and Owl came flying out of the Hundred Acre Wood to see what was wanted.

"Owl," said Christopher Robin, "I am going to give a party."

"You are, are you?" said Owl.

"And it's to be a special sort of party, because it's because of what Pooh did when he did what he did to save Piglet from the flood."

"Oh, that's what it's for, is it?" said Owl, helpfully.

"Yes, so will you tell Pooh as quickly as you can, and all the others, because it will be tomorrow?"

"Oh, it will, will it?" said Owl, still being as helpful as possible.

"So will you go and tell them, Owl?"

Owl tried to think of something
wise to say, but he
couldn't, so he flew
off to tell the others.
And the first person
he told was Pooh.

"Pooh," he said.
"Christopher Robin
is giving a party."

"Oh!" said Pooh.
And then seeing
that Owl expected him to say
something else, he said, "Will there
be those little cake things with pink
sugar icing?"

Owl felt that it was rather beneath
him to talk about little cake things
with pink sugar icing, so he told Pooh
exactly what Christopher Robin had
said, and flew off to Eeyore.

"A party for Me?" thought Pooh to himself. "How grand!" And he began to wonder if all the other animals would know that it was a special Pooh Party, and if Christopher Robin had told them about *The Floating Bear* and the *Brain of Pooh* and all the wonderful ships he had invented and sailed on.

While this was
going on inside him,
Owl was talking to
Eeyore.

"Eeyore," said
Owl, "Christopher
Robin is giving a
party."

"Very interesting," said Eeyore.
"I suppose they will be sending me
down the odd bits which got trodden
on. Kind and Thoughtful. Not at all,
don't mention it."

"There is an Invitation for you."

"What's that like?"

"An Invitation!"

"Yes, I heard you. Who dropped it?"

"This isn't anything to eat, it's asking you to the party. Tomorrow."

Eeyore shook his head slowly.

"You mean Piglet. The little fellow with the excited ears. That's Piglet. I'll tell him."

"No, no," said Owl, getting quite fussy. "It's you!"

"Are you sure?"

"Of course I'm sure. Christopher Robin said 'All of them! Tell all of them.'"

"All of them, except Eeyore?"

"All of them," said Owl sulkily.

"Ah!" said Eeyore. "A mistake, no doubt, but still, I shall come. Only don't blame *me* if it rains."

But it didn't rain. Christopher
Robin had made a long table out of
some long pieces of wood, and they
all sat round it. Christopher Robin
sat at one end, and Pooh sat at the
other, and between them on one side
were Owl and Eeyore and Piglet, and
between them on the other side were
Rabbit, and Roo and Kanga. It was
the first party to which Roo had ever
been, and he was very excited. As
soon as ever they had sat down he
began to talk.

"Hallo, Pooh!" he squeaked.

"Hallo, Roo!" said Pooh.

Roo jumped up and down in his seat for a little while and then began again.

"Hallo, Piglet!" he squeaked.

Piglet waved a paw at him, being too busy to say anything.

"Hallo, Eeyore!" said Roo.

Eeyore nodded gloomily at him.

"It will rain soon, you see if it doesn't," he said.

Roo looked to see if it didn't, and it didn't, so he said "Hallo, Owl!" – and Owl said "Hallo, my little fellow," in a kindly way, and went on talking to Christopher Robin, and Kanga said to Roo, "Drink up your milk first, dear, and talk afterwards." So Roo, who was drinking his milk, tried to say that he could do both at once...and had to be patted on the back and dried for quite a long time afterwards.

When they had all nearly eaten enough, Christopher Robin banged on the table with his spoon, and everybody stopped talking and was very silent.

"This party," said Christopher Robin, "is a party because of what someone did, and we all know who it was, and it's his party, because of what he did, and I've got a present for him and here it is." Then he felt about a little and whispered, "Where is it?"

While he was looking, Eeyore coughed in an impressive way and began to speak.

"Friends," he said, "it is a great pleasure, or perhaps I had better say it has been a pleasure so far, to see you at my party. What I did was nothing. Any of you – except Rabbit and Owl and Kanga – would have done the same. Oh, and Pooh. My remarks do not, of course, apply to

Piglet and Roo, because they are too
small. Any of you would have done
the same. But it just happened to be
Me. It was not, I need hardly say,
with an idea of getting what
Christopher Robin is looking for
now" – and he put his front leg to
his mouth and said in a loud whisper,
"Try under the table" – "that I did
what I did – but because I feel that
we should all do what we can to
help. I feel that we should all – "

"What's Eeyore talking about?" Piglet whispered to Pooh.

"I don't know," said Pooh rather dolefully.

"I thought this was *your* party."

"I thought it was *once*. But I suppose it isn't."

"I'd sooner it was yours than Eeyore's," said Piglet.

"So would I," said Pooh.

"AS – I – WAS – SAYING," said Eeyore loudly and sternly, "as I was saying when I was interrupted by various Loud Sounds, I feel that – "

"Here it is!" cried Christopher Robin excitedly. "Pass it down to silly old Pooh. It's for Pooh."

"For Pooh?" said Eeyore.

"Of course it is. The best bear in all the world."

"I might have known," said Eeyore. "After all, one can't complain. I have my friends. Somebody spoke to me only yesterday."

Nobody was listening, for they were all saying, "Open it, Pooh." And of course Pooh was opening it as quickly as ever he could, but without cutting the string, because you never know when a bit of string might be Useful. At last it was undone.

When Pooh saw what it was, he nearly fell down, he was so pleased. It was a Special Pencil Case. There were pencils in it marked "B" for Bear, and pencils marked "HB" for Helping Bear, and pencils marked "BB" for Brave Bear.

There was a knife for sharpening the pencils, and indiarubber for rubbing out anything which you had spelt wrong, and a ruler for ruling lines for the words to walk on, and inches marked on the ruler in case you wanted to know how many inches anything was, and Blue Pencils and Red Pencils and Green Pencils for saying special things in blue and red and green. And all these lovely things were in little pockets of their own in a Special Case which shut with a click when you clicked it. And they were all for Pooh.

"Oh!" said Pooh.

"Oh, Pooh!" said everybody else except Eeyore.

"Thank you," growled Pooh.

Later on, when they had all said "Goodbye" and "Thank you" to Christopher Robin, Pooh and Piglet walked home thoughtfully together in the golden evening, and for a long time they were silent.

"When you wake up in the morning, Pooh," said Piglet at last,

"what's the first thing you say to yourself?"

"What's for breakfast?" said Pooh. "What do *you* say, Piglet?"

"I say, I wonder what's going to happen exciting *today*?" said Piglet.

Pooh nodded thoughtfully.

"It's the same thing," he said.